Adventure
in
AMERICA

Adventure in AMERICA

BY

HELENA WELCH

SOUTHERN PUBLISHING ASSOCIATION

NASHVILLE, TENNESSEE

FOREWORD

Two of the most exciting adventures in American history stem from the discovery of gold in California and the opening of Indian lands for settlement in the territory of Oklahoma. Although these events took place forty years apart, a thrilling similarity exists between the two—one a race for wealth, the other a race for land.

The actual experiences of some of the children who took part in these adventures form the basis for the two stories related in this book. May their courage and faith in our heavenly Father be a source of inspiration to the boys and girls who read these pages.

CONTENTS

Gold in California

Introduction

The discovery of gold in California in 1848 came about quite by accident. Men had found gold in small quantities a few times before, but not enough to cause families all across America to beg or borrow the money for prairie schooners and to start the great trek to the gold fields.

The prairie schooners were large wagons covered with canvas canopies and drawn by mules or teams of steers called oxen. The journey from the eastern part of the United States to California in such a wagon usually involved much hardship, sickness, and misfortune.

However, the chills and fever, the difficult mountains, and the burning desert stopped only a few of the hardy travelers. The glitter of gold dust in the pan and the anticipation of the next shovel of sand striking pay dirt urged the forty-niners on.

The forty-niners—the people who journeyed to the California gold fields—made the journey because a man named James W. Marshall happened to pick up a small rock while supervising the building of a sawmill on the American River, not far from the present-day city of Sacramento. Mr. Marshall worked for Captain John Sutter and managed the huge estate called Sutter's Fort.

The early pioneers in California could have called Sutter's Fort the hotel of the West. Captain Sutter made his home a resting-place for travelers and welcomed all to stay as long as they wished. Its sprawling acres provided food and shelter for the many who came.

The new sawmill needed to be built as quickly as possible, and Mr. Marshall spent much time checking the work. One afternoon late in January, while on his rounds, he chanced to see a glittering stone amid the shale thrown aside from where the men worked on the dam.

Quickly Mr. Marshall asked for a tin plate and began washing the sand from the dam's diggings. It wasn't until the next day, however, the twenty-fifth of January, 1848, that Mr. Marshall told anyone that he had discovered gold.

The news spread among the sawmill workers and on to other villages and towns. Soon many wanted to try their hand at digging for gold instead of holding down a regular job.

To the rest of America the news traveled slowly. Sam Brannan, the publisher of a newspaper, *California Star*, had the greatest responsibility for letting the people east of the Mississippi River know what went on in the West. He prepared a special issue of his paper in March, 1848, telling of the gold discovery. Travelers took the issue east, and the excitement began.

"Wealth awaits the adventurer" became the slogan of the

people, and in the spring of 1849 many attempted to be adventurers. Some traveled by ship around Cape Horn at the tip of South America. Others took the route across the Isthmus of Panama. But more than forty thousand men, women, and children braved the trail by land across the western half of the United States. It was the harder route, even though the least expensive.

The children in our story traveled the overland route. Not among the forty-niners, they made the trip the next year. However, a year's passing had not lessened the dangers or the hardships of the trail. Their journey was much the same as that made by the actual forty-niners.

Trail of Courage

CHAPTER ONE

"TOMORROW! Tomorrow!" Betsy sang, skipping around the room. Then she raced to the big straight-backed chair where grandfather sat, and threw her arms around his leathery neck. "This is what I'm going to do when father comes home tomorrow. It's been such a long time since I've seen him." Her eyes sparkled with happiness.

Grandfather smiled and hugged Betsy. "Ten months has been a long time all right," he agreed. "Your grandmother and I will be glad to see him, too."

"And you aren't the only ones!" Jamie, Betsy's older brother, who had just come into the room, spoke up. "It has seemed as though he would never return from his trip to California. I can hardly wait to hear all about the trip west and back, and about the gold rush, and the—the forty-niners. Isn't that what they call the people who went to California to find gold?" He brushed his long hair away from his eyes.

Grandfather nodded. "Yes, son, that's right. But don't get your hopes too high. Sometimes our plans have to change because God has other things for us to do. When your father left, he had great plans. He spoke of a dream that he and your mother had before she died. Sometime, and somewhere, your father wants to make that dream come true."

Jamie's eyes grew wide, and he edged closer to grandfather. "But he'll come back tomorrow, won't he? You'll meet him at the stage stop, Grandfather, won't you? And what was the dream? Please tell us." Their grandfather had never mentioned father's dream before.

Grandfather shook his head. "It's up to your father to tell you about it. If he comes tomorrow, I'm sure he will tell you, but——"

Betsy looked as though she were about to cry. "Oh, Grandfather, he *must* come tomorrow!" she exclaimed. "It's been so long. Why wouldn't he come home? He told us he would. He promised to come back and tell us all about California and the gold rush."

"I know," grandfather comforted, putting his arms around both the children. "Grandmother and I want to see your father as much as you do. But enough of that now. Scoot off to bed so you'll be fresh and bright if he should come tomorrow."

Early the next morning Jamie scrambled down the wooden stairs, making a great deal more noise than usual. "Betsy, get up! You don't want father to find you asleep, do you?" he called as he passed his sister's room.

A giggle from below startled Jamie. Betsy poked her head through the faded parlor curtains. "I've been up for over an hour," she bragged. "And I even have the parlor all dusted."

Jamie frowned. "Why? Father won't care about dusting. He'll be too busy telling us about California to even notice if things are dusty or not."

"I guess you're right. But grandmother will like it." Betsy brightened. "She says we should always dust the parlor when company is coming."

"But father's not company!" Jamie protested. "He lives here."

"I know he used to live here with us," Betsy sighed. "But he's been gone for so long. I can hardly wait to see him again."

"Me, too." Jamie suddenly glanced around the room. "Where's grandfather? Isn't it about time for him to start to meet the stagecoach?"

"Why, he's already gone to meet it." Betsy laughed at her brother. "You were the sleepyhead this morning instead of me." Then she grew serious. "Father will come, won't he? Grandfather must have been wrong in saying that father might change his plans."

After a thoughtful silence, Jamie answered, "Yes, I think he will come. But—but I'm not as sure as I was yesterday. I'm wondering about the dream grandfather mentioned. I never heard father and mother talk about any special plans."

"I didn't either," Betsy added. "And I always listened when they talked together."

Jamie nodded. He knew Betsy had listened to their parents' conversations, but she was only five years old when their mother died of a fever. At that age she wouldn't have understood or remembered any serious plans if she had heard them.

Drawing a deep breath, Jamie looked up at the big clock on the wall. "Betsy!" he shouted. "Look at the time. Father has already arrived on the stage. He and grandfather are on the way home now!"

Betsy ran to the window and glanced at the frozen, rutted road. She seemed to bounce up and down with excitement. "Let's put on our wraps and wait in the yard," she suggested. "There we can see grandfather's buggy coming down the road."

Swiftly Betsy ran to get Jamie's coat and her own shawl from the hall closet. Even though it was early April, the Missouri wind nipped at ears and noses. Outside, small patches of snow still lingered along the rough brick walk, and pale sunshine played hide-and-seek with the ragged spring clouds.

Jamie had always been glad that his grandfather's house sat beside a quiet road away from the noisy hustle and bustle of Saint Joseph, but now he wished that it didn't take so long to drive from town. At last he heard the hoofbeats of Pacer, grandfather's carriage horse.

Also hearing them, Betsy looked down the roadway. "They're coming!" she cried. "Here come father and grandfather." As she spoke, the buggy rounded a curve in the road.

Jamie's heart stood still with disappointment.

His sister stared at the buggy and choked back a sob. "Father must have missed the stage," she wailed. "We will have to wait all week for the next one."

But Jamie knew when he saw grandfather's face that father wasn't going to be on any of the stages. The boy ran to the buggy as it came to a stop in the driveway. He swallowed the sudden lump in his throat and tried to speak, but no words came.

Grandfather understood. Leaning across the seat, he held out a long white envelope. "Your father didn't come, son," he said gently. "But he sent this letter by his good friend Mr. Simpson. Mr. Simpson will be by later to talk with us, but right now I know you and Betsy want to read your letter. While you open it, I'll put Pacer in the barn."

Without a word Jamie took the letter. Betsy crowded close to his shoulder as he tore open the envelope and slowly, haltingly, read aloud the closely written pages inside:

"Dear Children,

"I know this letter will come as a surprise and a disappointment to you, as you were expecting me to come home. But often the Lord leads us to change our plans. As much as I long to see you, I feel that I must stay here at Mok Hill— the shortened name of this mining camp, Mokelumne Hill.

"I know your mother and I never discussed a dream that we had with either of you because you were too young to understand. But we had planned someday to build a church in a place where the message of our Saviour's love had never been told. California is just such a place.

"Because this is a rough country, I want you to remain with your grandparents awhile longer. When I have my church built, I will send for you. Meanwhile I am sending this letter with my friend, Mr. Matthew Simpson, who is returning to Saint Joseph to guide a wagon train through Indian country back to California.

"Before I close, I send you both my love and ask that you do me a favor by sending something to me by Mr. Simpson. In my trunk you will find a box tied with a red ribbon. Give the contents to Mr. Simpson, except for the little blue leather purse. Keep it for yourselves. When I send for you, you will need what is inside.

15

"Take care of yourselves, and pray every day for our Saviour's blessing.

"Your loving father"

When Jamie finished the letter, Betsy seized his hand. "I know where father's trunk is. It's in the attic. Let's go see what's in it right now!"

For a moment Jamie hesitated. Somehow he didn't like the idea of going up to the dark, dusty attic alone. He wanted to wait until grandfather returned from the barn. But as Betsy tugged at his hand, he finally agreed. "All right," he said.

Betsy raced into the house ahead of him and darted toward the attic stairs. On the first-floor landing Jamie paused to glance again at his father's letter. While he stood reading, suddenly a bumping sound and a sharp scream came from above.

"Betsy!" Jamie took the steps three at a time, his heart thumping with fright. "Betsy, are you all right?"

From the dimness of the attic Betsy didn't answer. What had happened to her? Where was she? Jamie wondered. And did her scream have anything to do with father's trunk?

CHAPTER TWO

AT THE DOORWAY of the attic Jamie paused for a second, shouting his sister's name again. From the landing below he could hear grandmother calling, asking what had happened.

Jamie answered back that he didn't know, and peered through the musty dimness, trying to locate Betsy. As he brushed aside a tangle of spider webs, he heard a smothered laugh.

"Betsy, what happened?" Jamie rushed forward to see his sister lying in a tumbled heap on the floor. "Did father's trunk fall on you?"

"No!" She giggled. "I haven't even reached the trunk yet. At first I thought someone struck me, but I just ran into grandmother's dress form."

"Betsy!" Jamie didn't know whether to feel relieved or to be angry. His sister had frightened him half out of his wits, and now she was laughing about a dress form. She did look funny though, lying on the floor with it on top of her. Jamie extended his hand and was helping his sister to her feet just as grandmother came through the door.

Almost out of breath from her fast climb up the stairs, she gasped, "What happened, children? What was that terrible noise? And why are you up here? I thought you were downstairs waiting for your father."

"We were, but father didn't come home." Quickly Jamie explained about the letter and about Betsy's knocking over the dress form while searching for the trunk.

After being assured Betsy wasn't hurt, grandmother turned toward one of the big windows. "Your father's trunk is over here," she told the children. "I'm sorry he didn't come back from California. But if the Lord wants him to do His work where he is, then he certainly must stay."

The two children watched as grandmother lifted the lid of the old trunk. The box tied with red ribbon lay on top of some old clothes. "Open it, and see what's inside," grandmother suggested.

With eager fingers Jamie pulled on the ribbon bow and removed the top of the box. Inside nestled two books—one a large Bible, the other a songbook. Underneath the books lay the blue leather purse.

"We're to give the Bible and the songbook to Mr. Simpson," Jamie explained to grandmother. "And we are to keep the purse. Father said we would need it when he sent for us to come to California."

Grandmother nodded. "I watched your father put money in that purse the day before he left. He told me then that it was for you."

Wide-eyed with wonder, the children opened the purse

and stared at the many gold and silver coins. They had never seen so much money before. After a moment Jamie held out the purse to grandmother. "Take care of it for us, please," he said solemnly.

"All right," grandmother said as she took the purse and tucked it inside her apron pocket. "I'll put it in a safe place until you need it. Now let's go downstairs and find out from your grandfather about Mr. Simpson, who is to have your father's Bible and songbook."

Grandfather couldn't tell them much about Mr. Simpson. He had talked with him only briefly. "I do know, though," grandfather said, "that he is an honest man, and I like him."

If grandfather liked Mr. Simpson, then Jamie and Betsy knew they would like him, too. No one could judge character as well as their grandfather. When Mr. Simpson came later in the evening, both children ran to meet him.

"Well," the heavily sun-tanned miner greeted them with a twinkle in his eyes. "You might be my own niece and nephew back in New York. Why don't you call me Uncle Matt as they do?"

"We would like to, Uncle Matt!" Betsy exclaimed.

And for once Jamie was glad to go along with his sister's decision.

After the children had given Uncle Matt the Bible and songbook, he told them about their father. "He pans for gold along with the miners during the day and holds religious services at night. He has nearly worn out the Bible he brought with him, and he has no songbook. He sings hymns to us from memory until we learn them. Some of us sing pretty well, believe it or not." Uncle Matt smiled a bit at his statement, and the children laughed with him.

19

As Jamie and Betsy talked with their new friend, a warm feeling in their hearts, Uncle Matt's face suddenly grew serious. "Your father hasn't had an easy time," he told them. "Some of the miners are a rough lot. They laugh at and curse your father, but many are turning to the Lord because of your father's strong faith."

"I wish we were there to help him," Betsy said wistfully.

Mr. Simpson patted her curls with a work-roughened hand. "Someday you will be," he comforted. "Now it is enough for your father to know you're happy here with your grandparents."

Uncle Matt talked for a while about the wagon train he was planning to guide back to the gold fields. Then he left for the night. After he had gone, Jamie went to his room. Even though he was tired, he could not sleep. He kept thinking about his father, the money in the purse, and Uncle Matt's wagon train. Thoughts formed in his mind as he tossed. Toward morning he dozed with a plan in mind that he intended to discuss with Betsy.

Jamie didn't want grandfather and grandmother to know about the plan just yet, so he waited until Betsy had gone into the backyard to feed her chickens.

At first his sister didn't quite understand what he meant. "Of course, we're going to California," she insisted as she scattered grain to the rooster, Shadrach, and the cackling hens. "Father said in his letter that he would send for us when he has the church built."

Jamie shook his head. "No, Betsy, I mean we should go now—with Uncle Matt and his wagon train."

Betsy's eyes grew as big as the blue cornflowers that bloomed in grandmother's garden during the summer months.

"Jamie Blake! Where did you get such an idea? Uncle Matt would not let us. Besides, you know he said last night that everyone who joined his wagon train had to pay their way. How could we pay ours?"

Jamie grinned and tweaked his sister's nose as he always did when he was teasing her. "Think, Betsy. What did father say to do with the money in the blue purse?"

Betsy nodded slowly. Then her cheeks paled with apprehension as she thought of something else. "But it will be dangerous. There are the Indians. The wagon train is going across Indian country."

"We will be safe with Uncle Matt," Jamie assured her. "He is a friend of many of the Indians."

By the time Jamie and Betsy left the chicken yard, they had settled in their minds that they would go. It took a lot of persuading to convince grandfather and grandmother and Uncle Matt, though. The adults mentioned every danger or reason they could think of to discourage the children. At times Jamie and Betsy themselves felt almost too scared to go. But they did not give up hope. At last everyone agreed that now was as good a time as any to make the trip to the gold-rush country.

As eager as the children were to start, Uncle Matt told them the wagon train couldn't begin rolling until early May. Then the grass would be growing enough to feed the mules and oxen, and the weather would be favorable for traveling. Also the travelers didn't want to run into any late snowstorms. Twenty families joined Uncle Matt's train and camped on the riverbank to await the starting day.

The children would go with Uncle Matt in his large covered wagon. He and grandfather carried their father's heavy wooden trunk down from the attic and filled it to the brim with their possessions.

"I'll get the blue purse from grandmother, and father's Bible and songbook from Uncle Matt, and put them in here," Betsy declared as she folded a red-and-blue-dotted dress and packed it tightly in one corner of the trunk.

Jamie hurried to help grandfather build a special crate for Betsy's chickens.

When Uncle Matt came to put the children's things in his wagon, he grinned at the sight of the chickens. "Your new friends in California are going to appreciate these," he told Jamie. "They will pay a dollar apiece for fresh eggs."

Jamie gulped. The thought of so much money almost made him speechless. It reminded him of something he had to do. He must get the blue purse and give Uncle Matt the money for his and Betsy's fare. Jumping into the wagon, he lifted the trunk lid and reached for the covered box. But his hand touched only the Bible and the songbook. He could find no blue leather purse anywhere in the trunk. The money was gone!

CHAPTER THREE

JAMIE LEAPED from the wagon and sprinted toward the house. Inside the front door he shouted his sister's name. Betsy came flying out of the kitchen as fast as her long skirts would permit. "Jamie, stop shouting!" she scolded. "You know it isn't good manners."

At the moment Jamie was in no mood to worry about manners. "Betsy," he gasped, "the money is gone! The purse isn't in father's trunk!" He grabbed his sister's arm, ready to tug her out the door.

"I know that," Betsy answered calmly. "Grandfather and Uncle Matt discovered the lock was broken, so Uncle Matt put the purse in his trunk under the wagon seat, where it will be safe."

Jamie felt a little weak. "Why didn't someone tell me?" he groaned.

"I meant to," Betsy apologized, "but you were catching

the chickens. Then grandmother called me to help her bring more dried apples from the cellar."

Jamie felt a little foolish. He should have known that nothing would happen to the money, but it had been a shock to discover it was missing.

Soon Jamie recovered his old enthusiasm and entered into the final plans of packing. His grandparents had already stacked the wagon bed with boxes of clothing, food, mining supplies, and even a rosewood melodion covered with heavy canvas.

"The miners love music," Uncle Matt explained, patting the beautifully carved wood. "I play a little. Not good, but enough to get by."

Beside the children's trunk and the melodion, grandfather stacked sacks of dried apples, flour, cornmeal, potatoes from the pit in the cellar, and grain for the chickens. "There won't be any food shortage at Mok Hill when this wagon arrives," Uncle Matt joked. Then he looked serious. "But it is still a long journey. And at times it will be a hard one. Are you still certain you want to come, Jamie and Betsy?"

"Yes!" the children chorused. They knew they wouldn't miss the adventure for anything.

"All right then." Uncle Matt climbed into the driver's seat. "Let's get started."

Jamie and Betsy knew that they weren't actually starting on the trail to California. Instead they had to join Uncle Matt's wagon train on the riverbank and wait for the ferryboat to take them across to the other side, but just the same they had to tell grandfather and grandmother good-bye. Tomorrow the ferry began running, and the wagon train would have to be ready to take its turn in crossing the river.

"Good-bye, Grandfather! Good-bye, Grandmother!" the children called. They waved for as long as they could see their grandparents standing in front of the house.

At last Uncle Matt drove the mules around the bend in the road, and Betsy drew a long breath. "I wish going to a new place didn't always mean leaving someone behind. It spoils the trip."

Uncle Matt nodded his head. "Yes, it does; but you know it is hard to keep looking at our cake after we have already eaten it."

Jamie and Betsy couldn't help laughing at the remark. And in a little while they didn't feel so sad at leaving their grandparents. They hadn't traveled the road to the river often, so they found lots of interesting sights.

"Look at all the pretty flowers," Betsy exclaimed, pointing to a tiny valley nestled near a grove of trees. "I didn't know so many were blooming this early. Grandfather's meadow has only a few Johnny-jump-ups and field daisies."

"The flowers are blooming over there because that is a sheltered spot with a southern slope," Uncle Matt explained. "Out on the open prairie the soil has absorbed the winter freezes, and it takes longer for growing things to awaken. That's why it would have been unwise to start on our journey any sooner."

When they reached the wagon train's campsite, the children stared in amazement. The campsite looked like a small town. Squads of tents and covered wagons nestled on the cleared spot. Herds of livestock grazed nearby, and blue-gray smoke wreaths from the campfires wafted like clouds.

"Are all these people in your wagon train?" Betsy asked. "There must be hundreds here."

"Yes, there are quite a few folks here," answered Uncle Matt. "Not all of them belong to my train though—just twenty families. But they are all going to California. The 'gold fever' is a mighty contagious disease."

The children had heard much about "gold fever" the year before. Every forty-niner had gold fever—the urge to go to California to prospect for gold. These prospectors had helped settle Mok Hill—where the children's father was—and a lot of other gold-mining camps, such as Shinbone Creek, Shirttail Canyon, Rough and Ready, Skunk Gulch, and other such places with less unusual names.

The children found that the people going to California had just as good a sense of humor as the people already living there. As Uncle Matt drove through the camp, Jamie saw a slogan printed on the side of a nearby wagon. It read, "California or bust." Another sign said, "Meet me at Sutter's Fort," and a longer one, "Gold dust, get ready. I've got my broom."

"Uncle Matt," Betsy declared, "we need a sign on your wagon."

"Yes," Uncle Matt agreed. "I've been thinking about one, but I haven't had time to paint it on yet."

"What is it?" asked Jamie.

"Since this is going to be a long, difficult trip, we are going to need God to help us." Uncle Matt paused, then said, "I thought of 'It will take prayer to get us from here to there.'"

"I like that," Jamie agreed quickly.

"So do I," Betsy added.

After Uncle Matt stopped at his campsite, the children enthusiastically spent most of the afternoon painting the slogan on the wagon.

The next morning the ferry began taking the wagons

across the wide Missouri River. Another train went ahead of Uncle Matt's. The children had watched so many wagons drive over the ramp onto the boat that they weren't at all alarmed as Uncle Matt began urging the mule teams forward. Their hooves clattered on the wooden planking of the ferry.

They were almost aboard when a swift breeze flipped a piece of white cloth under the feet of the front team, and they began backing up with fright. The wagon wheels whirled toward the edge of the ramp and the cold, muddy water.

"Jamie!" Betsy suddenly clutched the seat and screamed. "We're going into the river!"

CHAPTER FOUR

AS THE MULES struggled in their harness, other teams around them grew restless, Betsy's chickens cackled, and women screamed. The ferry began to rock up and down in the water as the animals and wagons shifted position. But Jamie thought of the slogan on the side of the wagon and began to pray. "Please, dear Jesus, stop the mules from backing into the river," he whispered. Uncle Matt desperately tried to calm the animals before they backed the wagons into the freezing water or overturned the ferry and spilled everybody into the river.

Then the miracle happened. The mules suddenly stood still and, at Uncle Matt's urging, started moving steadily onto the boat again.

Betsy drew a long, quivering breath. "I was scared," she confessed to Jamie, who sat beside her.

"So was I," her brother admitted.

"It was a little close," Uncle Matt stated with a slow smile. "But we are on our way now."

The boat slid smoothly through the rippling water, and the soft spring sunshine flecked the dancing little waves with diamond flashes. A hawk wheeled overhead, then flew out of sight. In the back of the wagon one of Betsy's hens, Toppy, started to cackle.

Uncle Matt, who had been checking the mules' harness for possible breaks, looked up and called to the children. "That hen knows how to be thankful," he said softly. "We should be, too."

Jamie and Betsy understood at once what Uncle Matt meant. They bowed their heads for a moment of gratefulness to God for His protection. When they finished the prayer, Jamie looked again at the painted slogan on the side of the wagon and was glad that he and Betsy had taken the time to put it there.

On the opposite side of the river the ferry tied up at the bank. The wagons rolled onto solid ground again. "We will try to follow the trail left by the travelers last year," Uncle Matt told the drivers. He had already appointed several men on horses to act as scouts, and sent them ahead of the wagons to find the trail. The wagons drawn by mules went first, with the slower ox teams following behind.

Jamie liked to sit in the back of the wagon, perched on top of the crate where Betsy's chickens rode. From there he could see far down the line of wagons. He wished grandfather and grandmother had come along. Soon, though, he heard a sound that made him stop thinking about his grandparents. Someone was playing a guitar and singing a catchy little song. Jamie listened to the words:

29

"Oh, Susanna!
Oh, don't you cry for me!
I'm on my way to California
With my washbowl on my knee!"

Betsy had also heard the singing. She crawled over the seat where she had been sitting with Uncle Matt and joined Jamie. At the word "washbowl," she laughed. "That's clever," she remarked.

Following a pause in the singing, Jamie joined the singer with a stanza of his own:

"Cal-i-fornia!
You're the land for me!
There's plenty of gold, I've been told,
In Cal-i-for-ny-ee!"

At the end of Jamie's song, the guitar playing stopped, and applause sounded from the second wagon behind them. A red-haired boy of sixteen sat in the driver's seat, but instead of holding the reins, he cradled a guitar. Seeing that he had Jamie's attention, he grinned and clapped with all his might. His smile seemed to split his freckled face wide apart.

Jamie stood up and bowed. The man and his wife in the wagon directly behind Uncle Matt's smiled and began to sing the words Jamie had made up. In a few minutes singing burst out from all the wagons and continued until time to camp.

"I think we've started a happiness trail," Betsy remarked to Uncle Matt as they wearily climbed out of the wagon.

Uncle Matt nodded. "Yes," he said. "We'll need happiness along with courage on this trail. I hope we will have plenty of both."

"Looking around at the wagons that now formed a circle, Jamie and Betsy saw the red-haired boy a short distance away. At their call he waved and started toward them. "Won't you have supper with us?" Betsy invited. "My grandmother sent enough pies to last a week."

"Not with my appetite," the boy teased. "My name's Jack Horner, and I don't pull plums out of Christmas pies. I just eat them."

"And that makes you a good boy!" Laughing, Uncle Matt carried on with the nursery rhyme. "Welcome, Jack, to our wagon train. Bring the rest of your family, and eat with us."

The boy's face grew serious. "I'm my family, sir," he said. "There were only my older brother, Tom, and myself. We had planned ever since last spring to go west, but six weeks ago Tom took pneumonia. Now, only I am left."

"Sorry, son." Uncle Matt put his hand on Jack's shoulder. "We're glad to have you in the wagon train."

Jamie was especially happy to meet Jack. The twenty families making up the wagon train included a number of children and several boys, but none with the friendly, open manner that Jack had. "Are you going to Mok Hill?" Jamie asked hopefully.

"Tom and I never decided on any certain place," Jack replied. "We just wanted to find a spot where the diggings would be good, and I've heard they're good at Mok Hill. Is that where you folks are headed?"

"Yes," Betsy chimed in. "Father is there now. He wants to build a church, and we're going to join him. Only he doesn't know it yet. We want to surprise him."

Jack smiled at her. "I know what a nice surprise that will be."

31

The chilly darkness of a spring evening covered the camp. Uncle Matt, Jamie, Betsy, and Jack crowded around the blazing campfire. Everyone talked until it was time for worship. Jack stayed for prayer, and he and Jamie knelt side by side. With a heart full of gratitude for his new friend, Jamie offered a special thanksgiving to his heavenly Father.

The next morning Jamie awoke with one thought in mind. He wanted to ride in Jack's wagon. "Of course," Uncle Matt agreed when Jamie asked permission. "Just don't fall out."

"I won't." Jamie grinned back. He ran over to Jack and volunteered to harness his friend's mule.

Jack's wagon weighed much less than Uncle Matt's, making it much easier to pull. The two teams of mules walked briskly up hills where Uncle Matt's four teams pulled hard. But the bumps were much more intense. Jamie found it difficult to strum Jack's guitar while sitting in the jolting seat.

"Get in the back and sit on my bedding," Jack told him when he noticed Jamie wince from pain after one extra-hard bounce. "The straw tick will cushion some of the rough places."

Jamie hadn't sat on the soft straw-filled mattress more than a few minutes when a fierce jolt threw him backward. The wagon underneath him seemed to rise up, then suddenly plummet downward. Rolling across the bedding toward the tail gate, he tried desperately to clutch the straps of the canvas covering, but his fingertips touched only the last one.

"I'm going to fall," Jamie thought in desperation as a final plunge threw him against the tail gate, and he felt it give way under his weight.

CHAPTER FIVE

JAMIE closed his eyes and tried to pray as he tumbled from the wagon. A split second later he hit the rutted ground, and thinking quickly, rolled clear of the oncoming teams. Wagon wheels crunched past a few feet from his head.

For a moment he lay in a clump of dried grass, gasping for breath and trying to remember what had happened. Then he heard excited voices and Jack and Uncle Matt calling his name. Slowly, with his head whirling, Jamie sat up. "Here I am," he managed to answer. "I'm all right."

Jack reached him first. His face looked pale under his freckles. "Jamie, are you sure you aren't hurt?"

Jamie shook off some of the dizziness and tried to grin. "I'm not hurt. But what happened? Did we hit a bump?"

Uncle Matt, who was examining the wagon, answered, "You hit a rut, a big one, and it broke the coupling pole on your wagon, Jack. Snapped it clean in two."

Jamie struggled to his feet and brushed himself off. A streak of mud crossed his forehead and smeared his cheek. "Well, I thought if it was a bump on the trail, it certainly was a good one!"

Several people from the other wagons had gathered by now, and they all laughed, relieved that Jamie had not been hurt. Jack, however, wasn't laughing. As soon as he was assured that Jamie was all right, he began to worry about his wagon.

"I'm sorry about this, Mr. Simpson," he apologized to Uncle Matt. "The man who sold my brother and me the wagon said that it was a good one."

Uncle Matt nodded. "It's a good wagon, Jack. This accident could have happened to any of our wagons. Don't worry. We're all set for such emergencies as this one." He turned to a man standing nearby. "Mr. Moore, drive your second wagon as close here as you can, please."

Jamie knew that Mr. Moore's other wagon carried equipment such as tools, spare wheels, coupling poles, ropes, chains, extra sets of harness, and all kinds of medical supplies that might be needed for emergencies.

While the men started to repair Jack's wagon, Betsy led Jamie to a small shade tree. "Are you sure you're all right?" she asked anxiously.

Jamie couldn't keep from laughing. "If I hear that question once more," he warned, "I'm going to bed and let you wait on me all the way to California."

"That's what you think!" Betsy shot back. "I'll have Uncle Matt stop at the first house we see and leave you."

Jamie's face grew serious. "We won't see any houses for a long time, Betsy," he reminded her. "We passed the last one yesterday. Uncle Matt says we have to reach Fort Laramie before we see anyone outside our own wagon train—except for maybe some Indians."

Betsy shuddered. Then she stared across the rolling plains. The tall grass rippled like waves on the water. Only a few scrubby trees dotted the lonely landscape. "Fort Laramie is many miles away, isn't it?" she murmured.

"Yes, it is. And California is even farther on from Fort Laramie. But California is where father is, and that's where we're going."

Betsy smiled, and a look of determination crossed her face. She glanced toward Uncle Matt's wagon. "With Uncle Matt's slogan to help us, we'll get to California and father all right," she declared.

Jamie reached out and squeezed his sister's hand. "I think we will, too," he agreed.

Mending Jack's wagon took much of the day. A full day's travel covered about fifteen miles, but the train made only six or seven miles by nightfall that day.

Travel across the plains proved to be easier and more interesting than Jamie and Betsy had thought. Wild birds, colorful clumps of flowers, and occasional herds of antelope helped break the monotony of the vast prairies. Of course, they saw no houses. And so far they hadn't met any Indians.

One morning at breakfast Jamie noticed that Uncle Matt's usually cheerful face seemed tense. He didn't talk and plan the events of the day as he always had before. When it came time for morning prayer, he asked God to watch over them in a special way.

As though Uncle Matt's mood was catching, others in the wagon train seemed sober, too. No one sang to break the monotony of travel. Betsy's chickens nestled quietly in their coop, and not even Shadrach stirred. Instead of riding in Jack's wagon, Jamie climbed aboard with Betsy and Uncle Matt.

Between times of speaking to the mules, Uncle Matt turned his head sideways as if he was listening. Once Jamie saw him hold his hand to his ear.

At last Jamie broke the silence. "Uncle Matt, what's wrong? What are you listening for?"

A small smile crossed Uncle Matt's tanned face. "I'm listening to see if I can hear the gold dust swirling in the pans out in California."

Neither Jamie nor Betsy laughed.

"You're worried, Uncle Matt," Jamie insisted. "I can tell. Are we coming to a bad trail or something?"

Uncle Matt shook his head. "No, Jamie, the trail will be fine for a while longer. But for some time I have been hearing what I think is a roar. I didn't want to mention it yet, even though it seems to be getting louder."

Jamie and Betsy looked at each other in amazement. They had heard nothing, and they wondered how Uncle Matt could hear now above the creak of the wagons and rattle of the harness chains.

"Do you think it might be a storm?" Betsy asked, glancing at the few clouds in the sky.

"No," Uncle Matt replied. "A prairie storm is bad, but we could stand one better than what I think is coming. In fact, I'm certain it's coming. I'm going to stop the wagons now so that we can prepare for it. There's a grove of trees just ahead. It should provide wood for a big enough fire."

His statement upset the children.

CHAPTER SIX

TO JAMIE it seemed that hours passed from the time he first saw the buffalo until the herd reached the fire blazing in front of the wagons. Great stifling clouds of dust swirled upward and mingled with the smoke until the sky turned a dirty gray. People shouted to each other, but no one could hear because of the terrific roar of the pounding hooves.

Jamie held onto Betsy's hand. His mouth was dry from the dust and from fear. Smoke stung his eyes. The two children stood close to Uncle Matt and saw the first of the buffalo pass near enough to the flames to be scorched. They traveled so fast that they were only a dusty brown blur, but they veered away from the fire, leading the rest of the herd with them. Jamie felt Uncle Matt's hand tighten on his shoulder. Looking up, the boy saw that the tension had left the wagon master's face, and he was smiling.

Relief flooded through Jamie with such force that his

knees trembled. He knew Uncle Matt's smile meant only one thing: the danger had passed; the fire was turning the buffalo.

"Betsy, we're safe!" Jamie shouted close to his sister's ear, hoping she could hear him above the pounding of thousands of hooves. Betsy seemed to understand. She smiled and relaxed. A second later Jamie saw that she was bowing her head, and he did likewise.

The danger had passed, but not the herd. The monotony of the noise and stifling dust made Jamie's head ache. People everywhere coughed and gasped for breath. Some of the men continued to throw wood onto the fires, and others tried to quiet the mules and oxen tethered together inside the circle made by the wagons.

After a while Jamie climbed onto the seat of Uncle Matt's wagon, where he could see better. Some of the dust had cleared by then, and he could plainly see the running animals. Soon Betsy joined him, and they watched until Uncle Matt said they had to go to bed. The herd seemed to have no end.

The stars twinkled overhead when Jamie awoke. For a few minutes he felt puzzled about something. Then he knew what it was. It was the silence. He no longer heard the terrible thundering of the buffalo herd. The buffalo stampede was over.

Nothing eventful happened on the trail during the next few weeks. The routine remained the same. Rising early, riding on the trail all day, and camping at sundown made the children realize just how far away California was.

"Will we ever get there?" Betsy sighed once.

Jamie put a finger to his lips. "Remember, Uncle Matt said that we needed courage on this trail."

Betsy's chin lifted. "I've got plenty!" she declared.

Jamie knew that she had. He hoped that he would always have as much.

Although the wagon train had traveled through the Indian land, the children had glimpsed only a lone rider now and then far away across the prairie. When they came to the land of the Comanche and Ute tribes, they began to see more. Often silhouetted against the skyline at sunset a band of warriors watched them. The Indians did not come near the camp, however, and the travelers did not fear them.

Soon Jamie and Betsy grew used to the Indians and did not even think about them. Instead they puzzled over the things they saw beside the trail. Every now and then they passed piles of rotted clothing, bedding, pieces of broken furniture, and rusty tools.

After a while Jamie asked Jack about them. "They were left by the wagons that came over this trail last year," Jack explained. "Mr. Simpson was wise when he advised us not to overload our wagons. The grass is getting shorter each day, and our mules and oxen have the rougher part of the trail yet to go. Because our wagons are lighter, we won't have to discard part of our supplies. All of us are carrying only what our animals can pull."

The trail did grow rougher and the heat more intense. The sun beat down on the sandy hills so fiercely that the grass seemed to turn brown overnight. The children had to place the chicken coop underneath the wagon. The heat affected the rooster, Shadrach, so much that several mornings he refused to crow. Dust covered everything and even got into people's mouths.

"It will be better next week," Uncle Matt reassured everyone. "We will cross the Rockies soon, and then we'll reach the Green River."

"I don't care what color the river is," Betsy joked, "just so there's water in it."

"There's water in it," said Uncle Matt, laughing. "We'll camp there for the Fourth."

Independence Day. The details of the trip had so occupied the children that they had forgotten about the approaching holiday.

"A flag!" Jamie mourned. "We'll need a flag, and we forgot to bring one."

It seemed no one had remembered to bring an American flag. The Moore family had a small cannon that they had intended to use to frighten the Indians. It could be fired, but who could celebrate the Fourth without a flag?

"We'll make one," Betsy announced to the adults one day. Her enthusiasm quickly caught hold. Several women did the actual sewing, but it was Betsy's idea—Betsy's and Jamie's. Jamie thought of using some of Toppy's white feathers for stars. When one of the men raised the flag on a pole chopped from a nearby grove of trees, the small fluffy feathers stitched to the blue cloth really did look like stars.

The day dawned clear with a brilliant sky and cool river breeze. Several members of the wagon train made speeches. Mr. Moore fired the cannon, and everybody spent the rest of the day in feasting and singing. Mrs. Moore had prepared pies for everyone from the sack of dried apples grandfather had sent, and Uncle Matt and Jack took turns playing the melodion.

After the celebration the wagon train spent several days resting and allowing the mules and oxen to catch up on some badly needed grazing. Crossing the sandhills had been hard, but the most difficult part of the journey was yet to come.

"We'll reach the desert before too long," Uncle Matt warned. "There will be little water for miles. What few springs we will find will be heavy with alkali, a substance that makes the water unfit for drinking. We will have to be careful with our water supply after we leave the Humboldt River."

The journey from the Green River to the Humboldt River passed without too much difficulty, and Uncle Matt and the other men made plans for crossing the desert. They stored water in every available vessel. To feed the animals, they cut grass, reeds, and heavily leaved tree branches. Uncle Matt again cautioned everyone to use the water and the feed for the animals sparingly.

For a few days after leaving the river they traveled during the day. But when the temperature soared, it became too hard for daytime travel. Then everyone stopped and rested in the shade of the wagons and started on the way again at sunset. Soon even night travel became difficult. The sand, scorched during the day, did not cool off, and the heat rose from it in smothering clouds. Betsy let her chickens roost on top of their coop instead of inside in order to catch as much breeze as possible.

One afternoon the water gave out. Betsy and Jamie had only one small drink apiece and gave the rest of their allotted amount to Shadrach and the hens. They didn't worry though, for Uncle Matt had told them they would reach water during the night.

Dusty and tired, at sunset the wagons pulled out of camp. Darkness soon crept over everything, a smothery darkness that seemed to grow hotter with each step. The mules and oxen pulled on hour after hour, and the people walked to lighten the wagons.

Then Uncle Matt shouted the glad news. "Water! Just ahead!" All along the wagons people took up the cry, creating so much confusion that Jamie almost didn't notice when his sister broke into a run. In a second she had left his side and disappeared into the pitch blackness beyond the small circle of light cast by Uncle Matt's lantern. Startled, Jamie cried, "Betsy, come back!"

For a few minutes only silence answered Jamie. Then came a high-pitched scream, followed by a moan of pain. His heart thumping with fear, Jamie sprang forward.

CHAPTER SEVEN

"BETSY!" Jamie shouted as he stumbled in the darkness after his sister. Behind him he could hear other running footsteps and knew that Uncle Matt and Jack were following. Soon the flickering light of the lantern cast bouncing yellowish shadows into the inky black space in front of him.

At first Jamie saw nothing but sand. Then the lantern light cut into the glistening pool, and beside it he saw Betsy's crouched figure and heard her sobbing

With no thought of danger to himself, he rushed to his sister. "Betsy, what happened? What hurt you?"

Turning, Betsy hid her face against his shirt. "Oh, Jamie," she cried, "this horrible water! We can't drink it—it's too hot. It burned my finger when I touched it."

Before Jamie could answer, Uncle Matt reached out and took Betsy by the arm. "Betsy, you shouldn't have run away into the darkness like that. You might have stumbled and hurt yourself or fallen into the pool. Yes, this water is hot. In fact, these pools are called Boiling Springs, but look! I'll show you something."

Lifting the lantern, Uncle Matt held it high and swung it in a circle. On either side of the pool Jamie could see long dark shapes, but he couldn't make out what the shapes were.

Uncle Matt began to explain. "Other travelers in years gone by built these troughs you see to pour the water in to cool. When they had all the water they wanted for themselves, they left the troughs so that later travelers could use them."

Smiling, Uncle Matt paused and patted Betsy's shoulder. "Now, don't worry," he told her. "We'll dip up the water and pour it into the troughs. Then we'll all take a nap. When we awake, we'll have fresh water to drink."

In the lantern glow Jamie could see that his sister had dried her tears, leaving dusty smears on her pale cheeks.

"I'm sorry," she said. "I'll stay by the wagons from now on. And I won't cry over hot water anymore, either."

Jamie led Betsy back to their wagon. As he started to spread the blankets for her bed over the still-warm sand, Shadrach stirred on top of the crate and, in rooster fashion, let everyone know it would soon be morning.

Jamie grinned in the darkness. "It's after midnight, Betsy. It's almost another day, and another day will bring us that much nearer to father."

Despite their parched tongues and burning throats, the children slept. When they awoke, just as Uncle Matt had said, the water had cooled. It didn't have a good taste because of the many minerals dissolved in it, but they gulped it thankfully. The animals also drank their fill, though the mules snorted and the oxen bawled when they took their first sip. Shadrach and the hens had their share, and Betsy returned them to their crate. She fastened a wooden bucket of water to its side.

The men sprinkled water on the dried-out wagon wheels and soaked the canvas coverings. For a few hours, travel was bearable. Then, as the heat became more intense, the pioneers had to camp once more.

At last they passed out of the desert country and climbed into the cooler foothills of the Sierra Nevada Mountains. For a few days the traveling became pleasant. The children began to enjoy the trip once more. Then climbing grew more and more difficult.

The trail, rough and filled with stones, slanted upward until it seemed impossible to keep the wagons from rolling backward. Everyone walked to lighten the loads, and some of the men helped push the wagons up the steeper hills.

The wagon train lost several days repairing wheels and snapped coupling poles. The Moores' wagon had two wheels come apart, and they had to be rebuilt, for none in the supply wagon would fit.

Jack and Jamie and Betsy enjoyed the woods when they were not on the trail. They listened to the different birdcalls and tried to identify the tall pine trees. Jack showed them how to find their way through the forest by observing the bark on the north side of the trees.

"I could walk right on through the woods to father if I could climb these hills," Betsy remarked, but was greeted by hoots of laughter from the boys.

One morning after the men had finished repairing the wagons, Uncle Matt surprised everyone by stating that they would rest instead of travel that day. "Tomorrow we will climb a small hill," he announced. "Today I think we need to let the animals eat and get prepared for their hard job."

Surprised, Jamie spoke up. "A small hill! But, Uncle Matt, we've already climbed big ones. Why do we have to get ready for a small one?"

Although Uncle Matt's eyes still held their twinkle, he looked serious. "It will be one of our biggest obstacles yet, Jamie," he answered. "Tomorrow we will go through the pass. It will take some doing to get the wagons all up to the top and over. We'll have to double the teams and take only a few wagons at a time."

For a long moment no one spoke. Then Jack asked, "We'll make it; won't we, Mr. Simpson?"

"Of course," Uncle Matt assured them. "God has helped us so far. He will also help us through the pass and over."

The day crept by slowly for Betsy and Jamie. They tried to play games and make small talk with Jack. As soon as darkness fell, everyone retired. But the children didn't feel ready for sleep. Anxious, they could not stop thinking about climbing Uncle Matt's "small hill."

Before sunup the camp came alive. The women had prepared enough food for the day the evening before. As soon as everyone had eaten, the men harnessed the best teams. They hitched two extra teams along with Uncle Matt's mules. The men decided to take the heavier wagons up first while the teams were fresh. Oxen could pull some of the smaller wagons to give the mules a rest later. Uncle Matt's wagon would lead the way.

"Let's go up with our wagon, Betsy," Jamie suggested. They had planned to stay with Jack's wagon, but Jamie became impatient to reach the top of the pass. "If we go now, we'll see what's on the other side before anyone else does."

Betsy agreed. The children walked ahead of the wagons. Soon Betsy and Jamie both grew tired from the climb. They began to lag. Betsy wore a painful blister on her heel, and at last had to ride to the top of the pass in the wagon. She watched the coop with Shadrach and the hens in it to make sure it did not tumble out of the wagon. The chickens could not stand up without falling over as the wagon jostled along up the rocky trail.

Several times the men rolled large rocks behind the wagon wheels to give the mules a few minutes of much-needed rest. Finally the steepness leveled out, and a few yards farther on Uncle Matt's wagon came to a standstill.

Jamie, who had up until now been tired from the long climb, suddenly ran to the wagon. "Hurry, Betsy; get out. We're at the top of the pass. Let's watch the other wagons come up."

The children found an outcropping of stone where they could sit and watch the rough trail below and see the wagons making their way slowly up to the summit.

It took quite a while for all the wagons to reach the top. After the first ones came up, Uncle Matt and the other men unhitched the teams and led them back down the pass to help pull more wagons up. But as soon as they had all arrived, Uncle Matt started his wagon across the high country. The trail was still rough and treacherous in spots. Both people and animals struggled and gasped for breath in the thinner air of the pass. But Jamie and Betsy felt a strange happiness. They were in California at last. After a short rest, each family hitched their own team to their wagon.

The wagon train lumbered on through the rough and rocky country. Sometimes the men had to roll huge boulders aside so that the wagons could get through. Betsy ran beside her brother as fast as her sore heel would allow her. They started down a canyon trail, but suddenly Jamie pulled Betsy to a standstill.

His eyes were wide. "Betsy, now what shall we do?" he whispered, staring over the edge of the cliff in front of them. "Uncle Matt must have made a mistake in coming this way. Why, just look at this drop-off! How will we ever get the wagons down there?"

CHAPTER EIGHT

JAMIE and Betsy shrank back from the edge of the canyon trail where they stood, wide-eyed and trembling, and clung to each other.

The boy stared down over the sheer wall and shook his head. "It must be all of ten or twelve feet down," he gasped. "I wonder if Uncle Matt made a mistake in taking this trail. It looks as if we'll never make it now."

"We'll make it," a voice said. The children, startled, turned to find Uncle Matt standing beside them, smiling.

"Uncle Matt," Betsy exclaimed, "our wagons can never get over this—this cliff, can they?"

"They will have to, Betsy," the wagon master answered. "This is the way that many wagons have gone on the trail to the gold-rush country."

The children could hardly believe their ears. "How?" they both asked.

Uncle Matt turned away from the edge of the cliff and motioned for the children to follow. He stopped beside a huge tree. "See the groove around this tree?" he said as he pointed.

The children looked at the gigantic trunk and saw a deep cut running through the bark on one side. "What made it?" Jamie wanted to know.

"Wagons going over the side there," Uncle Matt said.

Then, as the children looked more puzzled, he went on to explain more fully. "We will have to use ropes in letting the wagons down the steep slope. This tree will be our anchor post. You see, all the wagons before us have gone down over this 'cliff,' as Betsy calls it, by putting ropes around the tree. The constant sliding has cut the deep groove. Our ropes will make the groove a little deeper."

"My!" Betsy tried to laugh. "How am I going to get down? I think I'll need a rope myself!"

"Come on!" Uncle Matt laughed and ruffled Betsy's curls. "We'll start getting the wagons ready to lower down over the side. Then maybe we'll let you down last, so you won't wear out the rope!"

"Uncle Matt!" Betsy wailed in mock indignation as she seated herself on a huge rock to watch the men work.

The wagon drivers secured a rope to each wagon, then slipped the rope around the big tree, and finally hitched the mules to the end of the rope. The mules backed slowly, lowering the wagon. Friction made the rope and tree bark smoke. They put axle grease in the tree groove to help the rope slide better. It took quite a while to get all the wagons down, but at last the wagon train began rolling again.

That evening Uncle Matt had the people all gather together for a special time of thanksgiving. "Thank You, our heavenly Father, for helping us to California." He knew that God had helped them escape many dangers that had threatened other parties of pioneers.

"Are we close to father's camp?" Jamie asked Uncle Matt later after the people had gone to their wagons.

"No, not yet," Uncle Matt told him.

"But"—Jamie couldn't hide the disappointment in his voice—"you gave God thanks for our trip to the gold-rush country. Aren't we there yet?"

"Not quite. We still have some distance to go before we reach Sutter's Fort. From there we will go on to Mok Hill, where your father is; but at least the trail will soon become much easier. There aren't any more high passes to go over or deserts to cross."

All thoughts of anxiety, worry, and hardships soon vanished as the travelers came near the end of their trip. The men discussed plans for their "claims," the plots of land they intended to mine on. They also spoke of "cradles," "long toms," and "sluice boxes."

The children whooped with laughter when they heard the strange terms and shouted out loud when Jack told them his plans for building a "cradle." "What do you want with a cradle?" Betsy gasped. "You don't have a baby to put in it."

"This cradle isn't for a baby," he told her. "It's a long box that's used to wash gold out of the sand. I'm not sure I know just how to build one, but Mr. Simpson is going to show me."

Uncle Matt told the children more about the cradle and explained that the "long tom" and the "sluice box" were also devices used to wash the gold sand. "The bigger claims use the toms and boxes," he added. "You can wash much more sand in a day with them than with the cradle. When we get to the mining camps, you will see some of them in operation."

Jamie and Betsy had many questions about Sutter's Fort. Mr. Simpson told them that John Augustus Sutter, who had been a trader on the Santa Fe Trail, had settled the place. Sutter's Fort was on a huge estate having more than thirteen thousand head of cattle, many hundreds of acres of grain, a huge orchard, and two acres of roses.

"What a lot of roses!" Betsy mused. "Won't they be pretty in bloom?"

The roses weren't blooming when the wagon train pulled into the fort, but the children saw the garden and imagined how it looked in the springtime. They also saw how the miners used the cradles and heard over and over again how Mr. Sutter's foreman, James Marshall, had discovered gold when checking the work on a dam being built at the American River.

The members of the wagon train split up at the fort. The Moore family almost decided to accompany Uncle Matt and Jack Horner to Mok Hill. Then at the last minute they changed their minds and continued on to San Francisco. The other wagons rolled in different directions, each family seeking the part of the country where they thought the mining would be best.

As welcome as they had been at the fort, Jamie and Betsy were glad when Uncle Matt pulled onto the trail again. They knew now that each mile would bring them nearer to their father.

"Won't father be surprised!" Betsy chattered as she bounced up and down in anticipation on the wagon seat.

Jamie was as excited as his sister. Occasionally he wondered what their father would say when they arrived so unexpectedly at Mokelumne Hill. "He'll certainly be surprised at any rate," Jamie thought.

Mok Hill was a bigger place than they had anticipated. Tents and shacks built of old boxes and odds and ends of lumber made up the camp, but the dwellings stretched across the hills in all directions. Close by were the diggings, huge piles of discarded gravel from which the miners had washed out the grains of gold.

Men standing knee-deep in the muddy water of a stream paused to watch the wagon lumber past. Some recognized Uncle Matt and waved. "Hi, Mr. Simpson! Welcome back!" several called.

"There's our tent," Uncle Matt announced, turning the teams onto a narrow road that wound through the camp. Giving the children a big wink, he stopped before the tent. "Surprise!" he called out in a jubilant voice.

Hardly daring to breathe, the children waited. But no one appeared in the tent doorway. Then from behind the wagon a rough voice spoke, startling everyone. "If ye be lookin' fer Pastor Blake, he ain't here."

CHAPTER NINE

THE CHILDREN stared at the speaker. If they hadn't been so surprised at his words, they would have almost wanted to laugh at his appearance. His fuzzy gray hair stuck up all over his head as though he had recently been rubbing it with a towel.

He repeated his statement, even louder than before: "Pastor Blake ain't here."

Jamie came out of his trance. "Why isn't my father here? What's happened to him?"

"Yes, please tell us where Pastor Blake is," Uncle Matt added. "This is the tent that he and I shared before I went to Missouri to lead a wagon train here."

A grin broke through the scraggly whiskers. "Well, I declare! Yer Cousin Matt! The pastor spoke 'bout ye often."

Extending a gnarled hand in greeting, the old man caught sight of Betsy. "Oh-h, and yer Betsy! I'd know them

56

gold'n curls anywheres. Yer pa's talked 'bout ye so much."

Betsy broke into a sob. "Where is my father?" she demanded. "Is he ill?"

"My lands, no! Don't be upset. Yer father's fit as a fiddle." The old man beamed. "He's just gone to the big city for some s'plies."

Jamie guessed that "s'plies" meant supplies. "When will father be back?" he queried.

"I 'spect he'll be back t'morry," the old man replied. "He wanted t' be here fer the Sabbath services. But climb outa that wagon! After travelin' fer such a spell, I know ye's tired. Sorry yer pa ain't here to welcome ye, but I'll do it. I'm Prospectin' Pete. Always prospectin' even if the gold dust's all petered out!"

Pete laughed at his own joke until Uncle Matt and the children joined him. In a few minutes everyone had climbed out of the wagons, and Jamie introduced Jack.

Then Pete discovered Shadrach and the hens. "Lands sakes!" he exclaimed. "Ye'll have to keep them chickens penned up. Folks 'round here ain't seen a fowl in so long they're likely to steal 'em. They's worth more'n gold dust!"

"We'll build a pen," Jamie promised quickly. Neither he nor Betsy could stand the thought of losing their pets now after bringing them safely such a long distance.

With Jack's help, Jamie soon built a pen out of scrap boards and placed it on the grass growing beside the tent.

When Betsy began taking the hens out of the wagon, Toppy wouldn't budge from the corner of the coop. "Come, Toppy!" she coaxed. Suddenly, as if she were answering Betsy, Toppy began to cackle.

After a few seconds a smiling Betsy climbed out of the

wagon with Toppy under one arm and something brown and warm in her hand. Marching over to Pete, Betsy placed the object in his hand.

"An egg!" he yelled, his voice spreading across the camp. "A real egg! I ain't seen one in years. I'd 'most forgot what one looked like!"

While Betsy told Pete he could have the egg, the other miners close by hurried over and began putting in their orders for eggs at a dollar each. Some even offered as high as two dollars. Word passed through the settlement, and before long everyone in Mok Hill had learned of Toppy's egg.

Jamie grinned at his sister's excitement. "You have a cackling gold mine of your own, Betsy!" he told her.

As soon as the chickens were settled in their pen, the children went with Jack to help him stake a claim. Jack did a lot of looking and finally chose a plot of land near Pete's diggings. Jamie helped drive the wooden stake in the ground with Jack's name on it. Jack still had to register the land in the mining office, but for now the stake showed it belonged to him.

When they returned to the tent, Jamie remembered something. "Betsy," he said, "we must get father's Bible and songbook from Uncle Matt's wagon. We'll want to give them to father as soon as he returns tomorrow morning."

Betsy nodded. "There's something else we have to get, too. I have them packed separately from our other clothing. I'll give you yours as soon as I get them unpacked." Then she went inside their tent.

Jamie's brow wrinkled in a thoughtful frown. What had Betsy packed that he didn't know about? Shaking his head, he went in search of Uncle Matt and asked him to open the box under the wagon seat. When Mr. Simpson lifted the lid, Jamie could see the still-filled blue purse. "Uncle Matt, you haven't taken your pay for our trip."

Uncle Matt's eyes twinkled as he patted Jamie on the shoulder. "Don't worry about that. I've got a little surprise of my own for your father tomorrow, and it all concerns that blue purse."

Jamie felt a little let down as he took the Bible and the songbook and carried them to the tent. First Betsy kept secrets from him, and now Uncle Matt had one.

He stepped inside the tent and saw his best suit draped across a bench. It was a little wrinkled, but freshly brushed. "Betsy! So that's your secret. I wondered if grandmother had packed it."

"I remembered my best clothes, too," Betsy hurried to say. "I packed them especially for us to wear tomorrow when father comes."

Jamie put down the Bible and the songbook and hugged his sister. "I can hardly wait for tomorrow."

The next day dawned the same as any other day at Mok Hill. Jamie and Betsy awoke to the aroma of breakfast being cooked over the campfires.

"Come and try some of this gold juice," Jack invited, waving a jar of molasses as Betsy and Jamie came over where he sat eating hotcakes. "Pete says it cost a dollar a pint."

The molasses was good, but Jamie looked puzzled as he tasted it. "Why," he said to Jack, "it doesn't taste any better than the kind that cost fifteen cents a gallon back in Missouri."

After breakfast the children put on their best clothes and prepared to wait for their father inside the tent until he had greeted Uncle Matt. When they heard his wagon coming, they scrambled quickly through the flap, leaving Pete, Jack, and Uncle Matt to meet him.

They couldn't help peeking through the tent opening as their father climbed from the wagon. "Oh, he looks just the same!" Betsy squealed, squeezing Jamie's hand so tightly that he winced.

"Of course he does!" Jamie whispered back. "But keep your voice down."

Jamie had a good reason for wanting Betsy to be quiet. He had just seen Uncle Matt give his father the blue purse.

Mr. Blake stared at Uncle Matt. "But—but the children were supposed to keep this until I sent for them!" he stammered.

Uncle Matt smiled. "They gave it to me for a purpose," he said. "And now I'm giving it to you to help build your church. I also have a melodion and your Bible and songbook. But inside the tent is the best surprise of all. In fact, two of them." Raising his voice, Uncle Matt called, "All right, surprises! Come out now!"

The children didn't need to be called a second time. Who reached their father first, no one could say. Everyone talked, but no one heard anything that was said.

Then Uncle Matt said, "These pioneers traveled a hard trail, but they had lots of courage."

The children's father nodded, his face shining with the joy he felt in his heart. "I know," he said. "Thank you for bringing them over the trail of courage. And now let us thank our heavenly Father for His many great blessings. Tomorrow will be the best Sabbath I've ever spent at Mok Hill."

Land in Oklahoma

Introduction

"There's no place like home," goes a line of John Howard Payne's old song. But suppose, like some of our ancestors of a century ago, we had no homes. Suppose people had no land to build on and no grass to pasture their animals on.

Strangely, our great-grandparents faced just such a problem. As our nation grew from the original thirteen colonies, its inhabitants settled more and more land. People moved on to other areas. When a region became heavily populated, people moved again.

To provide the different tribes of Indians with land of their own, the government forbade people of other races to move onto the Indian lands. For many years the land that now makes up the state of Oklahoma belonged to the Indians.

When the surrounding states became settled, people began to learn of the beauty and fertility of the Oklahoma lands and wanted to build homes there. Of course, the government could not allow them to do so without securing permission from the Indian tribes.

In March, 1889, however, the government persuaded the Indians to sell the land on which they were not living, an area called the unassigned lands. Immediately, President Benjamin Harrison issued a proclamation which declared that the lands were to open for settlement on April 22, 1889.

The government decided that the best way for everyone who wanted land to get it was to literally "run for it." Those wishing to be in the "land run" had to gather on the territory's border on the opening day and wait for the twelve o'clock starting time.

The authorities barred no one. They welcomed anyone who wanted to find a home. The only rule they made stated that everyone must start at the same time. There could be no "sooners," people who wanted to cross the border before the government opened the land for homesteading.

On a bright, clear spring day fifty thousand homeseekers listened for the noon signal that would send them racing across the waving green prairies. Among them were the children whose adventure is told on the following pages.

A Claim for Carl

CHAPTER ONE

CARL pushed open the schoolhouse door and ducked his head against the blast of icy Kansas wind that stung his cheeks. "You go home, Carrie," he told his twin sister. "I'm going to wait for Dick at the flagpole. He wants to tell me something."

Two big dimples flashed in Carrie's cheeks. She had bigger dimples when she was displeased than when she smiled. "Oh, you and Dick!" she snapped. "You've always got some kind of secret to tell each other."

Carl slowly shook his head. "It's no secret this time. At least, I don't think it is. Dick was trying to tell me during the spelldown something about a 'land run,' but Miss Turner saw us. He sounded excited."

"I don't see anything to be excited about," Carrie said with a frown. "What did he mean by 'land run,' anyway?"

"I think it has something to do with the Indian lands in

64

the Oklahoma Territory that grandpa and Uncle Jim are always talking about," Carl answered. "But I don't see why Dick would be interested in land that far away."

"Neither do I." Carrie sighed. "And I'm not going to stand around in this cold wind to find out."

Carl almost wished he hadn't promised Dick he would wait, either. But he had. Turning his back to the north, he drew his coat tighter and tried to think about last summer's bright sunshine.

Before long he heard Dick's cheery whistle. "Am I glad you waited, Carl!" he exclaimed. "I know you didn't hear a word I was saying during the spelling match."

"How could I with Miss Turner glaring at us as she did! But let's not stand in the cold. We can talk as we walk. What were you trying to tell me about a land run?"

"That's it!" Dick cried. "We're going to stake a claim in the land run in the Oklahoma Territory. That means we'll get some land just by racing for it. We're going in a covered wagon, and father is going to build a church. We're going to be real pioneers in a new land, just like the Pilgrims coming to Plymouth Rock in the history book."

Carl carefully listened to every word his friend said, but he wasn't happy. He didn't want Dick and his little sister, Saralee, and their parents, Pastor and Mrs. Randolph, to move away. The Randolph family had been kind to him and Carrie ever since he and his twin had come to live with grandpa and Uncle Jim after the train accident killed their parents.

With difficulty Carl swallowed the lump that had come up in his throat. "When are you going?"

"I don't know," Dick answered. "Father said the run

will open sometime in April, but he wants to start in plenty of time to make the trip."

"I wish I could go with you," Carl said wistfully.

Dick stopped quickly. "Why don't you?" Then he looked away. "No, I guess maybe you couldn't get any land. Maybe they allow only families to compete for land. But still, you're the only family Carrie has. That is, of course, besides your grandfather and your uncle. Maybe they would go stake a claim."

"Uncle Jim would never leave his store," Carl declared. About grandpa, he couldn't say. No one ever knew exactly what grandpa was going to do.

The boys had reached the crossroad, and Dick turned onto the path that led to the Randolphs' parsonage. Looking back at Carl, he tried to grin. "I surely wish you could go with us to the new land."

Carl managed to smile back. "I do, too," he said. "And who knows? Maybe I will."

As Carl walked on toward his uncle's store, his smile faded. The gloomy clouds overhead matched his mood. He longed to live on a farm once more. Although he and Carrie were happy with grandpa and Uncle Jim, never a day passed that he didn't remember the farm his parents had owned. Closing his eyes now, he could see the big reddish cows in the pasture, the fields of rolling golden wheat, and the crimson-cheeked apples that tasted so sweet after the first frost.

The farm was gone now. After the accident Uncle Jim had thought best to sell the farm and put the money in the bank to draw interest until Carl and Carrie were old enough to need it.

Carl took a deep breath. He knew Uncle Jim had done

the right thing. But he missed the farm. If only they could get one in Oklahoma! Even as he thought about it, though, he knew it was hopeless. He couldn't go to Oklahoma by himself. And he couldn't ask Uncle Jim to go, because of the store. Still, there was grandpa. Grandpa helped Uncle Jim every day in the store, but somehow Carl didn't think he liked the work. Once he had said to Carl, "I like to see things growing in the ground with the sun shining down on them, not staying hidden in sacks and cans on wooden shelves."

Suddenly Carl's heart began beating faster. He could ask grandpa, he thought with mounting excitement. Maybe he would like to go to the new territory. Carl broke into a swift run. The frozen crust of old snow felt hard and sharp under his boots, and the icy wind flung scattered snowflakes into his eyes. But he didn't mind the cold now. He only ran faster.

"I hope Carrie hasn't told grandpa anything about Dick and the land run," Carl thought to himself. But he was almost certain she hadn't. As soon as she reached the store, Carrie usually went upstairs to the living quarters to study for a while before she helped grandpa cook supper.

In a few minutes Carl turned onto the street where his uncle's store was located. As he slowed down for a heavy dray wagon to pass, he caught sight of something that caused his throat to tighten with fear.

Thick black smoke poured out the side door of the grocery in great puffs. Desperately Carl raced around the dray wagon. The store was on fire!

CHAPTER TWO

BY THE TIME Carl reached the front door, he was gasping for breath. But with a fresh burst of strength, he rushed inside, making the little bell on top of the door chime loudly.

"Carrie! Grandpa! Uncle Jim!" he shouted. "Where are you?"

Above the chiming of the bell, his grandfather answered, "Over here, helping your uncle struggle with this spiteful stovepipe! Don't tell me the smoke is so thick you can't see us!"

Once inside, Carl could see his grandfather and uncle plainly. There wasn't as much smoke as he had thought. And what there was floated toward the open side door, leaving the air in the store nearly clear. "Whew! I thought the store was burning!" he panted. "That smoke was really pouring out into the street. What happened? Did the stovepipe fall down?"

By now grandpa and Uncle Jim had the pipe back in place. Grandpa climbed down from the box he was standing on and shook his head. "Nope! At least, it didn't fall without help from me."

Uncle Jim stepped off his chair and patted grandpa's shoulder. "You didn't knock the pipe down, Dad," he comforted. "That stack of boxes just tumbled against it."

"That's right!" grandpa agreed, stroking his moustache. "And who stacked the boxes so that they would tumble? Me. Give me a shovelful of dirt, and I can coax any green plant to grow. But stacking boxes and measuring beans in sacks —huh!"

"Would you like to have a farm, Grandpa?" Carl almost shouted.

Grandpa's blue eyes twinkled at Carl over the rims of his glasses. "I surely would." He smiled. "But that's something you can't buy in this town."

"But you can get one in the Oklahoma Territory!" the boy exclaimed.

Uncle Jim, who had been wiping soot from the stovepipe, looked at Carl with an amused expression. "Why this sudden interest in the Oklahoma Territory?" he asked. "The other day when your grandfather and I were talking about President Harrison's proclamation for opening the new land, you said it would just mean more history to learn."

Carl ducked his head in embarrassment. Until today the news about the land run had just seemed like so much history. Talking with Dick had changed that.

Before Carl could answer Uncle Jim, his grandfather spoke. "You think you would like to go to this new country, Carl?"

"I know I would!" Carl answered. "Pastor Randolph and his family are going. Dick just told me."

Grandpa nodded. "Yes, Pastor Randolph told me they have been thinking about it for some time. I'm glad they have decided. In fact, I've been doing a little thinking of my own."

Suddenly grandpa turned to Uncle Jim with a teasing smile. "I believe you could run the store better without my being here to burn it down, Jim. I think Carl and I just might go to Oklahoma ourselves. Would you like that, Carl?"

"Would I! Yippee!"

Uncle Jim's grin broadened. "Go ahead, Dad," he beamed. "You and Carl will make great pioneers."

"Carrie will make a great pioneer, too!" Carl added, racing for the stairs. "I'm going up right now to tell her we're going to Oklahoma."

During the next few days Carl never stopped racing, it seemed. He had many things to do in such a short time. Grandpa and Pastor Randolph bought two teams of mules and two covered wagons. Carl remembered the wagons his father had used on the farm, but the new ones were different. Painted a bright green with red wheels, they had large canvas coverings stretched over the tops.

"They will hold all our supplies," grandpa declared. But when loading time came, it seemed doubtful that the wagons would. Carl and grandpa had to squeeze in food, bedding, extra clothing, feed for the mules, and seed for planting.

At last, though, they had everything ready—at least Carl *thought* everything was ready. "We must wait for Johnny Walking-Stick," Pastor Randolph surprised everyone by saying.

"Who's he?" Carl asked, wide-eyed.

"He's the Indian guide I hired to help us get to the new land," Pastor Randolph replied. "There's a lot of country between here and there, with only broken trails to follow. We

70

might take the wrong one and be too late to enter the land race."

Carl nodded and prepared to wait for Johnny Walking-Stick. But somehow he didn't think he would like the Indian. He remembered all the stories he had heard and read about Indians harming people, and he wished that Pastor Randolph had hired someone else for a guide.

Two days later Johnny arrived. To Carl's surprise, he saw a tall boy of about nineteen with friendly dark eyes and a quiet smile. "But I don't care how friendly he looks," Carl thought to himself, "I still don't like him."

Because of the smallness of the Randolphs' cottage, Uncle Jim invited Johnny to spend the night at the store. "I'll just spread my blankets on the floor," Johnny said.

Carl felt rather sad when he went to bed for the last time in his room above the store. Somehow, now that the time for leaving had almost come, he hated to go. He was thinking how he would miss Uncle Jim and all his friends, and then he dropped into a light doze.

Suddenly Carl jerked wide awake. A strange noise floated up the stairs. Alarmed, Carl sat up in bed, listening. Then he remembered that Johnny Walking-Stick was sleeping in the store. It must be he who was making the noise. But what was he doing?

CHAPTER THREE

CARL couldn't lie still after he had heard the strange sound. Slipping out of bed, he hurried toward the stairway. He was halfway down before he recognized the noise—the side door being slid slowly back. Uncle Jim seldom used the door, and Carl had rarely heard the creaking sound it made.

But why was someone opening it now? Uncle Jim always bolted it from the inside. It had to be Johnny Walking-Stick who was pushing it. Why was he leaving the store?

Carl hurried as fast as he could. But by the time he reached downstairs, the store was empty. A streak of moonlight showed the side door still open, and Carl moved carefully toward it. Stories of Indian treachery flashed through his mind.

In the vacant lot beside the store, where the wagons stood with the mules chained to the hitching rods, Carl saw Johnny talking in a low voice to one of the mules and patting it gently. Puzzled, Carl watched. The mule stood away from the wagon as though the Indian had untied the rope and backed it up. Then, slowly, Johnny led the mule forward and tied it to the hitching rod.

Carl couldn't keep quiet any longer. Stepping out into the moonlight, he demanded, "What have you been doing with grandpa's mule?"

"Tying it to the hitching rod," Johnny Walking-Stick answered calmly. "It had slipped its halter and was about to wander away. By morning you would have had a hard time finding it."

Carl knew that what Johnny said was true. Once a cow had broken the pasture fence at home, and Carl's father had searched all the next day before locating the animal. "I'm glad you tied the mule back to the hitching rod," Carl told the Indian. "But how did you know it had slipped its halter?"

"I heard it snort," Johnny said. "A mule has a different sound when it's free."

In his room again Carl lay thinking about the Indian. At least, Johnny knew all about animals, he decided.

The next thing Carl knew, Uncle Jim was calling him. "Time to get started for Oklahoma!"

It was still dark, but Carl became wide-awake in a minute. He dressed quickly by lamplight and hurried to the kitchen, where Carrie and grandpa had breakfast nearly ready.

When Carl heard Johnny Walking-Stick climbing the stairs from the store below, he remembered the mule. He quickly told grandpa what had happened during the night.

His grandfather looked surprised. "Perhaps having Johnny along is going to help us more than I thought!" he commented.

When Johnny came into the room, grandpa thanked him.

"You've saved us from having to make a mighty big search," he added, shaking the Indian's hand.

By the time everyone had climbed into the wagons, the eastern sky glowed with a pale light. Pastor and Mrs. Randolph took the lead. Because Carrie wanted to be with Saralee, she rode in their wagon. Dick climbed up beside Carl and grandpa, and Johnny mounted his black pony.

As soon as everyone was settled, Pastor Randolph bowed his head for prayer. In his usual quiet way he thanked God for the privilege of moving to the new land and asked for help in making the journey safely.

After the prayer, Uncle Jim and the friends of both families crowded around the wagons to say good-bye. Even though the sun had not yet peeped over the horizon, half of the town had come to see them leave.

"Start the teams!" Uncle Jim shouted. "We're going to chase you right out of town."

And chase they did. Everyone raced down the gloomy streets, laughing and trying to keep up with the wagons. Now and then someone dropped behind. Others walked faster, but finally only Uncle Jim was left. "I won!" he said, laughing. "I ran halfway to Oklahoma!"

When at last he, too, had stopped and headed back toward town, Carl knew they were really on their way. The sun came up, and the wind rose sharply. "It's going to be a stinger today," grandpa commented as he held the reins with a firm hand. "We may have to walk part of the time to keep warm."

It wasn't long until Carl and Dick followed grandpa's suggestion. The brisk walk beside the wagon soon warmed them, and they climbed onto the seat again. They could see

A CLAIM FOR CARL

Carrie and Saralee wrapped in a feather bed in the back of Pastor Randolph's wagon.

"The girls are having a fine time," Carl told Dick above the rumble and rattle of the wagon.

"Yes," Dick answered with an absentminded nod. Carl saw that he wasn't paying attention to Carrie and Saralee. He was watching Johnny Walking-Stick astride his shiny black pony.

Dick grinned when he saw Carl looking at the Indian, too. "Don't you wish you could ride the way he does?" he remarked.

"Yes," Carl admitted. But he really wasn't too interested in the guide. He spent most of the morning gazing across the countryside.

They had left the town behind now, and the houses grew farther and farther apart. By lunchtime they were far out on the frozen prairie.

Carl thought he had never tasted anything as delicious as the soup Mrs. Randolph had prepared the night before. She had kept it warm all morning by placing the covered kettle on hot bricks and wrapping it all in quilts. "I wish your mother's soup would last all the way to Oklahoma. It's so good!" he told Dick.

"So do I." Dick grinned back.

The men fed and watered the mules during the short noontime rest. By midafternoon the wagons left the main road and turned onto a cattle trail. It was rough, but the heavy wagons didn't bounce too much.

Shortly before sunset, Johnny halted in a small grove beside a stream. "Plenty of wood here for the night camp," he explained.

Mrs. Randolph cooked supper over a fire built in a shoveled-out pit. "It's just like an all-night picnic!" little Saralee exclaimed while they ate, her eyes shining with glee.

"Yes," Carl agreed. "But I certainly wouldn't want to stay up all night after all the traveling we have done today!"

Going to bed in the covered wagon seemed strange, but Carl slept soundly through the night. The stars were fading when he awoke. He lay still a moment. Then he sat up quickly, his heart pounding. From somewhere out in the gray stillness came a terrifying moan.

CHAPTER FOUR

CARL CLUTCHED the blankets with shaking fingers. "Grandpa! Dick!" he whispered. "Do you hear that?"

No one answered. Carl could barely see their sleeping faces in the dim early-morning light. He listened again. The moan sounded louder and seemed to be coming from the other wagon. Johnny Walking-Stick, the Indian, was Carl's first thought. Had he hurt someone in Pastor Randolph's wagon?

Swiftly Carl pushed aside the covers. As he did so, grandpa and Dick awoke. When grandpa heard the moans, he looked worried. "Something is wrong for certain," he murmured. "I think it may be Saralee or Carrie who is moaning."

A stab of fear went through Carl's heart. Not Carrie, he kept praying. He didn't want anything to happen to anyone, but especially not to his sister.

As though in answer to his prayer, Carrie suddenly ap-

77

peared at the side of the wagon. "Saralee is sick, Grandpa!" she cried through chattering teeth. "Pastor Randolph thinks she has a fever of some kind. He wants to turn back to town and take her to a doctor as soon as we can."

Grandpa nodded. "That will be best."

But another voice cut in sharply. "No! The little girl must not be bounced over the rough trail." Johnny Walking-Stick came to stand beside Carrie. "She needs to rest and to drink the tea from the herbs I will find."

Herbs! In freezing weather? Carl could hardly believe his ears. "How can you find any kind of herbs now?" he asked skeptically. "There's nothing growing this time of year."

"I will find them," Johnny declared in a quiet voice. "Have the pastor to wait. I will return soon."

Already the Indian was striding toward his pony. He did not take time to saddle it, but swung up on the animal's bare back. Everyone watched as he rode away in the shadows. Then Carrie and Dick hurried away to take Pastor and Mrs. Randolph the message.

"Well, lad, I guess we'd better build up the campfire." Grandpa put a warm hand on Carl's shoulder. "Everyone should have some breakfast. And don't worry. I think Johnny knows what he's doing."

"I hope so," Carl answered as he hurried to gather wood and help grandpa with the camp chores. After breakfast they could do nothing but wait. Mrs. Randolph stayed in the wagon with Saralee. Carrie and Dick sat by the fire, but Carl couldn't stand being still. He kept moving around the wagons, petting the big mules and watching down the trail.

The sun traveled slowly across a cloud-studded sky, and a March wind whipped sharply. Saralee moaned and tossed in the Randolphs' wagon. At noon there still was no sign of Johnny Walking-Stick. When Pastor Randolph, his face pale with anxiety, said grace, he spoke a special prayer for Saralee. Silently, Carl prayed one of his own. He asked God to help Johnny find the herbs he needed.

The answer to Carl's prayer came in midafternoon. He had just finished taking the mules to water and had brought them back to the wagons. As he tied their ropes, he heard a sharp sound that caused his heart to pound—the hoofbeats of a horse galloping at top speed. Carl knew it was Johnny even before he caught sight of the black pony.

The pony flashed into camp, its wet sides heaving. Johnny slid down near the fire with a tangled mass of brown roots in his hand. "Get one of your mother's kettles," he ordered Dick. "We must make a tea of these roots."

In a few minutes they had washed the roots and put them in a small quantity of water to boil. Carl and Dick brought more wood, and Carrie stirred the mixture in the kettle with a long-handled spoon. After a while the liquid turned dark. Johnny, who had been watching, said, "It is ready," as he turned to Carrie. "Get the little girl's mother."

After Saralee drank the liquid, she grew quiet and was soon sleeping soundly. "Now she will be well," Johnny assured them with a smile.

Everyone crowded around the Indian boy to thank him for the medicine, but he only shook his head. "I just want the little girl to be well," he said, and slipped away.

The medicine made from the roots broke the fever. In two days Saralee was well enough to travel. The wind had stopped blowing, and the weather had turned somewhat warmer. But even though it meant that they could shed their heavy coats, it also meant trouble for the wagons. The ground thawed, and at times the big wheels sank in the mud. To lighten the load for the mules, everyone except Saralee walked. They rode only when the teams had to cross the small streams.

One afternoon shortly after lunch they came to a larger stream. Its muddy brown water swirled from bank to bank in a never-ending torrent. Large tree branches hurtled down the racing current. Carl, who was walking a short distance behind Johnny, saw the Indian pause and study the stream for a moment. Then he lifted his hand.

"Everyone get in the wagons and hold fast," he commanded. "The mules will have a hard time in this one."

Carl climbed into the wagon with his grandfather and Dick. Grasping a fold of the canvas cover, he clung tightly with both hands. But as the wagon hit the water, the swift current swung the front wheels to one side, nearly toppling the vehicle over. Carl lost his grip and went tumbling into the icy rapids of the stream. As he fell, he heard Dick shouting.

Gasping, Carl tried to swim. But the cold water numbed his arms and legs until he could scarcely move. Then a whirling wave tugged him under. As he went down, he tried to pray.

From a far distance he heard someone calling, "Help! Carl is drowning! Oh, please save him!" The voice sounded like Carrie's. Carl wondered if he would ever see his sister again.

CHAPTER FIVE

AS CARL STRUGGLED frantically in the chilling water, he tried to pray. "Oh, please, Jesus, help me!"

He didn't need to pray a second time. A strong arm seized him and pulled him up out of the water so that he could breathe again. Gratefully, Carl gulped in the fresh air as someone dragged him to the stream bank.

"Bring blankets!" a familiar voice ordered. "And build a fire at once."

By then Carl could breathe freely enough to become interested in finding out who had rescued him. Looking up, he saw Johnny Walking-Stick, dripping wet, beside him.

The Indian's brown face broke into a smile. "The water is a little cool for bathing today."

Carl managed a weak grin. "You can say that again!" he whispered hoarsely. "Thanks for saving me. I'm sorry I fell out of the wagon and caused so much trouble."

"This kind of trouble I do not mind," Johnny answered.

In a few minutes Carl and Johnny sat wrapped in the blankets that Mrs. Randolph and Carrie brought from the wagons. And in a short while grandpa and Dick had a big fire blazing. When Carl and Johnny were warm and dry again, Pastor Randolph spoke. "Let's all give thanks to the Lord for answering our prayers and saving Carl. We should be especially thankful since we have seen God's protection twice so far during this trip."

Johnny was the first to agree. "Without the Saviour's help, I could not have swum with Carl against the current," he said.

Carl bowed his head with the others. But his prayer was different. Not only did he thank Jesus for helping save his life, but he also asked to be forgiven for distrusting Johnny.

They encountered no more large streams to ford, and the weather turned just right for travel. The trails grew dry, and new grass pushed up everywhere. Each morning found the prairie a shade greener than it had been the evening before.

One afternoon Johnny stood beside Carl as they fed the mules. "By tomorrow evening, if we make good time, we will reach the border of the new lands," the Indian said.

Carl could barely keep from whooping with joy. Having lost all track of time, he had no idea they were so near their goal. Yet they had been traveling for several weeks. In fact, he realized with amazement that it must be about time for the run to begin.

As though Johnny had read Carl's thoughts, he smiled. "The run is just three days away," he said.

Forgetting about the mules, Carl raced toward the campfire. "Grandpa! Carrie! Pastor Randolph!" he shouted. "We're almost to Oklahoma, and the run starts in just three days!"

A Claim for Carl

The children all had different ideas as to how the border would look. Dick asked Johnny to describe it, but the Indian just shook his head. "Wait and see," he said.

The next evening just before sunset the wagons came to a small hill. There the trail widened into a road that seemed to have had a great deal of travel. "Looks like quite a few folks may be going to the same place we are!" Grandpa chuckled and urged the mules up the hill.

At the top Carl suddenly leaned forward on the wagon seat. "Look!" he gasped, pointing to what seemed like a city of tents. "Is that the border?"

"Yep!" Grandpa chuckled again. "Yep, that's it."

As they drew closer, they could see wagons, horses, mules, dogs, and people moving in all directions. Several people waved a welcome and moved their wagons to make room for Pastor Randolph and grandpa to camp together.

When the wagons were settled, Carl shook his head. "I didn't think there would be this many people here. I wonder how they will all get in line when the race begins!"

"And I'm wondering if we are all going to start together," Dick added.

The boys' questions were answered two days later when everyone got ready for the big race. Troops mounted on horses patrolled the border and kept out the "sooners." The children thought the term sounded funny until they learned that "sooners" were people who didn't want to wait for the run to begin. They wanted to cross the border ahead of everyone else in order to get the best land.

"Everyone should have an equal chance," worried Dick, "but I don't see how they will. No mules or anything else can outrun that railroad train!"

The train Dick meant had just pulled up on the tracks near the border and stopped. (The Atchison, Topeka and Santa Fe Railway had fifteen such trains steamed up and waiting to cross into the former Indian lands.) People crowded the train inside and out, sitting on the top and clinging to the sides.

Johnny had been watching the train and listening to the boys' conversation. Now he told Dick, "Don't worry about the train moving too fast. They're supposed to run at a slow speed. When they come to a possible townsite, people will jump off and stake out lots. The people on them will have to run on their own feet to get their claims."

"Whew!" Dick exclaimed. "I'm glad I'm not riding on the train, then!"

But before Carl could agree with Dick, grandfather motioned for the boys to climb into his wagon.

It was nearing noon, and Pastor Randolph pulled his mules into line with grandpa's. For as far as Carl could see either way, teams and riders prepared for the final moment.

Under the warm April sun everyone suddenly grew tense. The shouting and laughter died away, and except for an occasional call, the border was quieter than it had been anytime during the past three days.

"How will we know when to go?" asked Dick.

Grandpa pointed to the mounted police. "The cavalrymen will fire their rifles."

"Then I'm going to plug up my ears!" Dick said. "When all those guns go off, the noise is going to be loud."

But Carl didn't care how loud the guns were. He wasn't going to cover up his ears. He had come a long way to be in the race, and he wasn't going to miss even the rifle shots.

Holding his breath, Carl waited. It was quiet now, like the hush before a storm. Horses and mules impatiently stamped, eager to be moving. Then the sharp cracking of the rifles split the air. The run was on!

"Hold tight, boys!" grandpa shouted as the wagon jerked forward up the slight incline.

"We are!" Carl yelled back. Then his eyes widened with terror. "Grandpa, look out! That wagon—it's going to crash into ours!"

CHAPTER SIX

FOR WHAT seemed hours Carl stared at the big yellow wagon careening wildly backward toward them. He realized that the harness must have broken, letting the team go free. No one rode in the wagon either, so the driver must have jumped out.

Dick tugged at his sleeve. "Duck, Carl! Duck down!" Carl knew that Dick meant for him to drop off the seat onto the bottom of the wagon bed, but he didn't. He closed his eyes tight and waited for the jolt of the crash. When it didn't come, he opened his eyes again.

The crowd had parted, and the yellow wagon had passed them. It was rolling backward toward the open prairie, where it could run without hurting anyone until some ditch or tree stopped it.

"Whew!" Dick climbed up on the seat, out of breath. But grandpa gave a deep chuckle. "It was close, boys!"

Carl didn't answer, but he wanted to tell his grandfather that he would rather not come that close to danger again.

In a little while, however, Carl forgot about the near accident. It was easy to see across the country now. Most of the other wagons had gone out of sight. The prairie lay like a green-and-brown carpet of new and dried grass. Clumps of colorful flowers dotted the green here and there. Before long Carl saw a pool of clear water that sparkled with the blue of the spring sky. "Look at the pretty lake!" he exclaimed to Dick.

"You mean lakes!" Dick corrected. "There are three more on this side of the wagon. I never saw so many lakes in one place before."

Johnny suddenly rode close enough to the wagon to hear Dick's remark. "Welcome to the land of the 'buffalo wallows,'" he said.

Carl was glad to see his Indian friend. In the excitement of the run he had lost sight of Johnny. "Why are the lakes called 'buffalo wallows'?"

"Because the buffalo herds made them," Johnny answered. "The animals pawed up the dirt to lick the salt in the ground. Then when it rains, the holes fill up with water."

What a strange and wonderful land Oklahoma was, Carl thought.

Just then Dick asked, "Will we see any buffalo?"

Johnny shook his head. "I don't think so. Most of the herds have drifted out of the Territory by now. That is, what is left of them. Hunters have killed most of the buffalo."

Before Johnny could tell the boys anything more, grandpa stopped the team. Just ahead Pastor Randolph had also halted. He pointed to a stream that rippled through a small grove of trees.

87

All at once Dick stood up. "Father has decided on the place to build the church!" he exclaimed. "Right over there by that grove."

Dick was right. Pastor Randolph drove to the spot and began pounding the stake with his name on it into the ground beside the stream.

With a bound Dick leaped out of the wagon and ran toward his father. For a moment Carl and his grandfather sat, silent and undecided. Then grandpa urged the team forward. "Well, boy! What are we waiting for! Let's put our stake down on that other claim over there before someone else beats us to it!"

Carl didn't need to be told twice. Before his grandfather had stopped the mules, he had climbed out with the name stake. Carrie had seen them and came running across the prairie from Pastor Randolph's wagon. "Grandpa," she cried, "we're home!"

For a moment grandpa only nodded his head. Then he put his arms around his grandchildren. "Yes, Carrie and Carl," he said softly, "we are home. We have our own claim now, our own land."

As soon as the children had explored the claim, grandpa told them it was time to start putting up the tent. "It will have to be our home until we can build a house," he explained.

Carl began to worry. He hadn't thought about a house before. He had been interested in land. Now he wondered what they would use to build a house.

When he asked, grandpa grinned. "Sod, boy! Just plain old grass. There are layers and layers of grass roots in this dirt. We plow up chunks of it and put them together."

"Just like bricks!" Carl replied. "We'll be using grass bricks."

"That's right," grandpa answered. "When the pastor and I get back from filing our claims at the land office, we'll start building our sod houses."

The next morning Pastor Randolph and grandpa decided to ride to the nearby townsite and have their claims put on record. Johnny, too, decided to leave. Now that both families had settled on their claims, they no longer needed him for a guide.

Carl had not realized how fond he had become of the Indian. The lump in his throat kept him from saying good-bye. And a little later he found Carrie crying. "We'll never see Johnny again!" she sobbed.

"No, I guess we won't," Carl agreed with her sadly.

All morning they worked inside the tent, arranging the things that grandpa had carried in from the wagon. At noon they ate lunch with Mrs. Randolph and Dick and Saralee. Then they hurried back to the tent to work some more.

They were still busy in the middle of the afternoon when Dick poked his head through the tent opening. "What are you two doing?" he asked. "I've been shouting at you for five minutes."

Carl looked up from the dishes he had been unpacking and frowned. "What for?" he demanded. "I know your mother invited us to come for supper, but it isn't suppertime yet."

"No, of course not!" Dick spoke impatiently. "But there's such a bad storm coming that mother wants you to come and stay in the tent with us."

"Storm!" Carl and Carrie both echoed, just as a rumble of thunder shook the ground under their feet. A moment later the three children raced across the prairie to the Randolphs' tent. Mrs. Randolph and Saralee waited for them.

"We must try to hold the flap shut," Mrs. Randolph cautioned, "or the tent may be blown away."

The boys helped her fasten the front part of the tent with small ropes. By now the wind had risen to a low whine, and drops of rain began drumming on the canvas overhead.

"We'll ask Jesus to keep us safe," Mrs. Randolph said.

Everyone prayed. Then the storm broke. Soon a torrent of icy water swirled over the floor of the tent, and blasts of raging wind tore at the flap. Suddenly the small ropes holding it gave away, and the flap flew wide open. As the sides of the tent lifted, Carl heard Carrie scream, "Oh, the tent is blowing away!"

CHAPTER SEVEN

CARL and Dick both ran to seize the tent flap, but the driving wind and rain forced them back. Then, swiftly, someone raced in out of the storm, clutched the tent flap, and pulled it shut with a firm hand.

For a moment Carl did not recognize in the darkened tent the soaked figure. Then he exclaimed, "Johnny! You came back!"

"Yes," the Indian answered. "I saw the storm coming and knew that Mrs. Randolph and you children were here alone. I thought you might need help."

"We certainly do!" Mrs. Randolph agreed. "In a few more minutes the tent would have blown away."

It seemed that the hardest part of the storm had struck just as the tent flap opened. The wind soon ceased, and the rain pelted less fiercely on the canvas overhead.

In a little while Johnny let go of the tent flap and stepped outside. At the same moment Carl thought about his tent. "Carrie, do you suppose our tent's been blown away?" he questioned. "There was no one to hold the flap shut."

"Your tent probably stood better than this one because of the little hill to the west," Johnny commented.

Carl had never liked the steep little hill, but now he was glad it was there. Comforted by Johnny's words, he hurried out into the still-drizzling rain. At the top of the hill he closed his eyes. When he opened them, he saw the gray canvas of his grandfather's tent still standing. Whooping with joy, he turned and ran back down the path to tell Carrie the good news.

The next day Pastor Randolph and grandpa returned. They had been worried about the storm. Pastor Randolph shook his head in amazement when Mrs. Randolph told him how Johnny had kept the tent from blowing away. "What will we do without him when he does leave?" he remarked.

As the day passed, however, Johnny did not mention leaving. "Maybe he is going to stay with us," Carrie suggested hopefully. "Let's ask him."

Somehow Carl didn't think they should. "If Johnny wants to stay, he will," he told his sister.

When work began on the sod houses, Johnny pitched in to help. Both grandpa and Pastor Randolph appreciated his aid. They had many things that seemed to need doing all at one time. The men had to build fences around the pasture for the mules and prepare land for planting, as well as plow sod and cut poles for the houses.

The children thought it a miracle that anyone could actually make a house from dirt. "I'm going to forget that I ever lived in a lumber house!" Dick laughed.

"I am, too," Carrie added. "I only wish I had the carved wooden motto that mother kept on the wall in our old house. It said, 'God bless our home.' If I had it, I would hang it on the wall of our new sod house."

Carl remembered the motto. He had wanted to take it when he and Carrie had left their home, but the people who bought the house had also wanted it.

"Maybe someday we'll have another motto like mother's," Carl told his sister.

Johnny had been standing nearby listening to the children. Now he smiled in a pleased sort of way and went back to his work.

The next day Johnny began acting strangely. Right after lunch Carl saw him slip away into the bushes by the stream. He slipped away often in the days that followed. Nearly two weeks passed before Carl learned what Johnny had been doing in his spare time.

By then the houses were nearly completed. The walls were made of sod and the roofs of poles and sod. The men smoothed off the hard-packed earth floors with a spade and swept them shiny clean. Only the windows and doors remained unfinished.

"We'll go to the townsite and get real glass windows and wooden doors," grandpa told the children. "The pastor and I will leave in the morning. We will be back in time to have our houses finished by Sabbath."

On Friday Carl and Carrie awoke before the eastern sky had turned pink. In the distance they could hear the early morning calls of the quails and larks, and they felt like singing along with the little prairie birds.

"By evening our house will be finished," Carrie said as she and Carl ate breakfast. "We'll have worship in our house."

"That's right," Carl agreed. "We can have something special at worship, too."

Carrie immediately wanted to know what it was, but Carl wouldn't tell her. "Wait until grandpa puts in the windows and doors. Then I'll show you," he promised.

By midmorning grandpa and Pastor Randolph arrived with the glass windows and the wooden doors. The twins helped put them up until grandpa started on the last window. Then Carl said to Carrie, "While grandpa is fixing the window, let's get the special something I found."

Carrie nodded, and the children hurried up the little hill. They hadn't gone far when Carl pointed to a clump of bright pink flowers. "There. Wild roses almost like the tame ones mother grew in our yard. Let's pick a big bouquet to put in our house."

For a moment Carrie just stared at the flowers. Then she ran happily forward. "Won't grandpa be surprised with the flowers!"

The twins each had an armful of the beautiful flowers when they heard Dick shouting from the top of the hill. "Carl! Carrie! Hurry. Your grandfather wants you."

A lump of fear rose in Carl's throat. Had something happened to grandpa? Seizing Carrie by the hand, he ran toward Dick. "Is grandpa hurt?"

"No," Dick answered. "He just said for you to come. I think he wants to tell you something about Johnny."

Johnny! Carl's heart skipped a beat. Surely his Indian friend was all right. Nothing must happen to Johnny.

As the children came in sight of the sod house, they saw grandpa standing by the door, holding something in his hand. Carl knew he must be mistaken, but the square object looked exactly like his mother's motto. Then he saw that it was a motto. Grandpa held it out to him and Carrie.

"Johnny left you this," grandpa said softly. "I guess he had a time working on it without our knowing about it."

Carefully Carl took the motto. Now he knew why Johnny had been slipping away from time to time. Carrie reached out to touch the polished wood of the motto. "We must thank Johnny right away!" she declared.

But grandpa shook his head. "You can't." Raising his arm, he pointed across the prairie.

Carl quickly turned to look. Far away he saw Johnny riding his black pony. As he stared, the Indian lifted his arm and waved. Blinking away the sudden tears in his eyes, Carl waved back. Then he felt his grandfather's hand on his shoulder.

"Someday our friend will return," grandpa declared. "I feel certain of it. And now we must get ready for the Sabbath so that we can thank our Saviour for both our home and our friend Johnny."

Carl and Carrie nodded. They knew that in their hearts they would always thank Jesus for letting them know such a friend as Johnny Walking-Stick and for allowing them to have such a wonderful new home in Oklahoma.